Connor, Callum & Noah,

May you have
Many Wonderful years
together with
Alexis —
~ Sandie + Donna
Axe
2002

The Adventures of Buddi The Greyhound

Finding a Family

Tara Tisopulos
Story

Rob Tokar
Art

For Laki, Alexa and Buddi, the three reasons why my world is such a wonderful place.

--Tara

For Eric, Julie, Danny, and Becky, who once said she wants to be an artist like her Uncle Rob. . . only better.

--Rob

The artist would like to thank Kevin Carr and Steve Buccellato for their coloring assistance and advice.

First Published in 1999 by Great Dog Publishing.

1 2 3 4 5

www.buddionline.com

Great Dog Publishing
P.O. Box 1388, Claremont, CA 91711
www.buddionline.com

"Attention all Greyhounds," a voice echoed
from the loud speaker into the kennels.

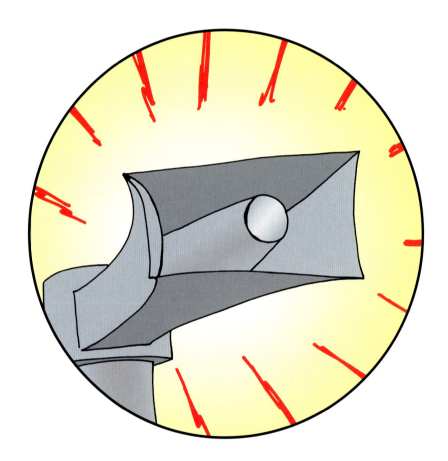

"Those of you who wish to retire from racing, please proceed to the exercise yard. Several families are already gathering who are interested in adopting racing greyhounds."

"Pssst, Buddi," called LeRoy Greyhound from his lower kennel, "What are you going to do? I'm thinking about giving this family-thing a try."

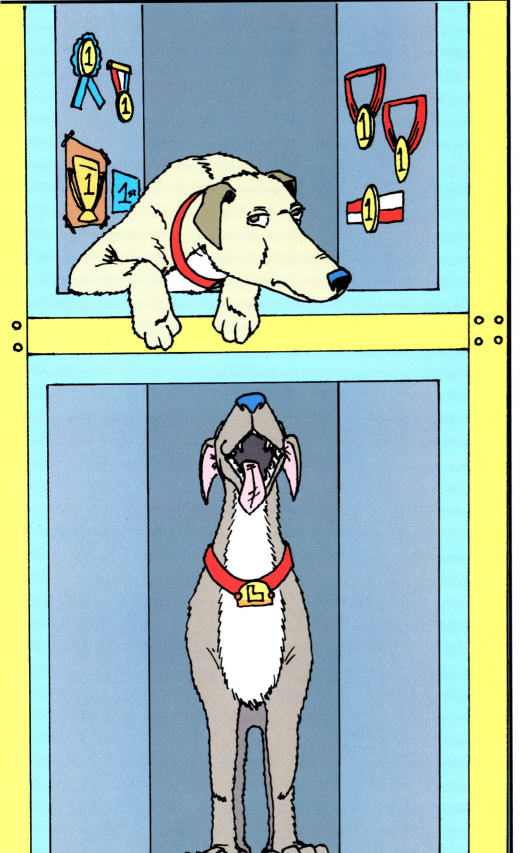

Buddi and LeRoy work at a dogtrack. They compete in races and win prizes if they come in first place. Buddi is the star of the track.

"I'm not even sure what a family is," said Buddi confidently.

"At the pace that you run, LeRoy, you don't have much choice but to retire. I, however, am an undefeated champion. Why would I leave?"

With that, he sat back down on his bed and rolled his eyes, bored by the very thought of a family. . . whatever that was.

"Just because you're undefeated now doesn't mean it'll last forever, Buddi," LeRoy replied, ignoring Buddi's insult about his speed.

"You're not a puppy anymore and you're not in very good shape. Speedy and Slim were telling me at practice yesterday that a new dog is being transferred to our track. Her name is Trophy and she's never lost a race, either. The track owner is bringing her to compete against you in Saturday's big race.

I think your winning streak is coming to an end. If you lose, you're never going to hear the end of it from the guys."

"Yikes!" thought Buddi.

He had heard of Trophy. She was famous in the racing gossip circuit. She was younger than Buddi, and skinnier, too. Could his perfect racing record be over? He'd never be able to face his friends again.

"Being a champion is all I know, he thought. How can I end my career as a loser?"

"Maybe I'll beat Trophy," Buddi speculated.

The race was six days away, however, and Buddi hadn't practiced or exercised in weeks. He knew he could beat all of the dogs at the track without any effort, so he never exerted himself.

He was lazy.

"Last call for retiring greyhounds," the loud speaker echoed again.

"That's it," Buddi thought. "If I retire today, I won't have to race Trophy. I'll leave the track with a perfect record. They can't call me a loser if I don't run in the race. I don't want to retire and leave racing now, but it's better than ruining my perfect winning streak."

"Wait for me, LeRoy," Buddi shouted, "I think I'm ready to retire, too!"

"What made you change your mind, Buddi?" LeRoy asked with a smile. "Did Trophy scare you away from your career?"

"Don't be ridiculous," Buddi said, "I could beat anyone. I've been thinking about retiring for awhile."

When Buddi and LeRoy arrived at the exercise yard, they were surprised to see several of their fellow athletes groomed and ready to meet potential families.

"I knew I should've taken a bath," LeRoy said. "I really want a family to adopt me. I've heard wonderful things about families. There are children who pet you and scratch those hard-to-reach spots behind the ears. There are warm places to sleep and there's good food to eat. Best of all . . . you can run just for the fun of it; not because you have to win."

It's not about winning in a family; it's about love.

"Whatever," Buddi thought, as he wandered over to the far corner of the exercise yard. He just didn't know if he was doing the right thing by leaving the track. He desperately wanted to keep racing, but only if he could keep winning. A family would be boring and silly but at least he'd be an undefeated champion. No, he decided firmly, he would not continue racing. His career was officially over.

Buddi was disgusted at the behavior of his colleagues as the families entered the yard. The dogs were barking, jumping and wagging their tails like common house dogs. Even LeRoy was getting in on the act. He was running around the yard with two little girls, chasing them and running to fetch a ball. They were hugging him and scratching his ears. His tail was wagging completely out of control. Buddi was embarrassed for him.

He stayed over in the corner of the yard, yawning and rolling his eyes.

Buddi looked up to see LeRoy being put on a leash and leaving with the two little girls and their parents. He stopped and ran over to Buddi before leaving.

"I've got the most amazing family, Buddi," he said. "I'm going to have a whole new life and I've never felt this happy before. My family tells me that they are going to take me to a dog park near our house. Maybe we can meet there."

"Go on, LeRoy," Buddi said nonchalantly, although inside he was very sad to see his friend leaving. "Give up your career to chase your tail."

"I have a feeling I'll be seeing you at the dog park, Buddi," LeRoy said. "Try family life, you could use a little love." With that, LeRoy disappeared to his new life.

Buddi resumed his scowl and curled up again in the corner of the yard. He fell asleep.

Buddi awoke only moments later to the sound of a young voice approaching.

"Mom and Dad," the little boy said. "Look at this dog over here all by himself. He looks sad. He needs a home, too."

"Here comes trouble," thought Buddi.

"I don't know, Alex. He doesn't look too friendly or playful," said the boy's father.

"That's exactly why we should adopt him, Dad. He needs us. The other dogs will all find families but this one probably won't. Buddi needs us to make him happy and to love him," said Alex after bending down to read Buddi's dog tag.

Buddi made no effort to get up and meet the family. Alex, however, was not dissuaded in the least.

"Come on, boy," he said, pulling Buddi to his feet and hugging him. "Do you want to live with us?"

Buddi barked his response, which was a firm "No."

"See that, Dad," Alex said, "He said 'yes.' He wants to live with us."

"Oh no," Buddi thought. "The kid doesn't understand dog language. I said... no, no, NO!"

"He certainly responded to you, Alex," his dad said. "If this is the dog you want, then this is the dog we'll adopt."

Alex quickly snapped the leash on Buddi and started leading him out of the yard. With head and tail down, Buddi was pulled out of his exercise yard, listening to the jeers and chants of his colleagues.

"Thought you were too good for a family, Buddi!" they sneered. "Trophy has chased you away."

He was so humiliated that he picked up his pace and little Alex could barely keep up with him. "See Dad," Alex said, "Look at how excited Buddi is to get to his new home."

Life for Buddi would never be the same.

Alex talked to Buddi the whole way home. Buddi, however, was deep in thought. All of the guys knew that he was afraid to race Trophy.

He hadn't left like an undefeated champion. He had crept away like a coward.

Buddi
was impressed with his new
home. He wasn't sure what a home was
because he had never left the track but this was
nice. There was softness under his feet that he had never
felt before. Alex told him it was called carpet. The house was
warm with big fluffy nap areas called couches and beds for the
humans. Alex told Buddi that he would be sleeping on his bed at night.
"Looks pretty good," Buddi thought. "It certainly beats the wire crate I
used to call home."

The best thing about home, Buddi decided, was the smell. Alex's mother laughed as
Buddi headed toward the source of the wonderful aroma. Alex said it was called the
kitchen and that mom was making her special beef stew to welcome Buddi into the
family. Beef stew smelled better than dry dog food!

After the delicious meal, the family settled down to watch television. Buddi headed
for a corner of the room but finally edged closer when he couldn't stand Alex's beg-
ging a moment longer. Buddi jumped onto the couch and lay down next to Alex.
Mom and Dad looked pleased and Alex was ecstatic.

"You'd think he just won the lottery," Buddi thought. He was an undefeated
champion, yet no one at the track ever got that excited when Buddi
entered the room. He felt good.

Buddi didn't know why, but he liked Alex. "This kid's not
so bad," he thought, as he snoozed on the couch.

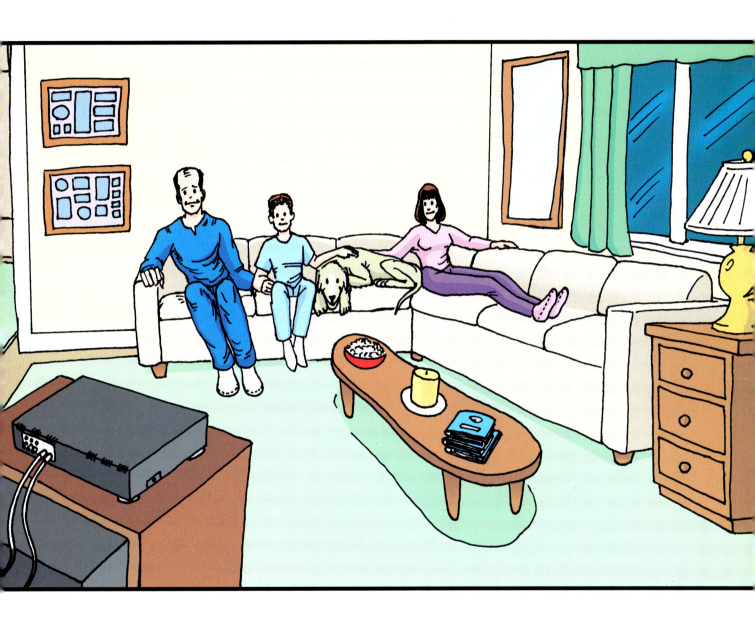

Buddi and Alex spent the next morning running through the backyard, which was green and hilly. Buddi was used to running on hard dirt, so it was a pleasant change to have thick, cool, soft grass under his toes. Alex was very impressed with Buddi's speed. He called his mom to come to the window and watch Buddi perform. Buddi was pleased. He was the fastest dog at the track, but no one there ever looked at him with such adoration or cheered for him like Alex did.

Evenings were spent walking through the neighborhood with Alex and his parents. Buddi had a new bright blue collar and matching leash and felt quite handsome. Neighbors were always stopping to say hello and to pet Buddi. They often commented on how sleek and elegant he was. He was so proud. Everyone at the track looked exactly like him, so no one there thought he was special.

"LeRoy was right," Buddi thought, "families are okay."

Buddi was happy with Alex and his parents but leaving the track with such shame was still bothering him. He found himself running the backyard in a big circle as if it were the track. When he wasn't running, he felt down and humiliated.

"Everyone must be laughing at me behind my back," he thought. "Trophy should be arriving today with no competition for Saturday's race. I could have beaten her," he thought. "Now everyone will think I was a chicken."

Alex noticed that Buddi seemed down. Running made him happy but being a part of their family didn't. Alex felt terrible. Buddi obviously missed running and wanted to be back at the track. As much as Alex loved Buddi, he knew what he must do.

Saturday morning, Alex and his parents put Buddi into the car.

"You're going home," Alex told Buddi. "I know that you are happier running in your races than being a part of our family. I love you, Buddi, but I want you to be happy so I'm bringing you back to the track . . . to your true family."

Buddi didn't know what to think. He missed racing. He had been running all week in his backyard so he thought he had a pretty good chance of beating Trophy. Now he could get back his self-respect with the other guys at the track. They had ridiculed him and called him a coward. He would show them.

Buddi's greyhound colleagues were shocked by his return to the track. "You're back, Buddi," they sneered. "We'll see who the top dog is today. Trophy is here and she's ready to race."

Buddi's trainer came running over and took Buddi's leash out of Alex's hand.

"Come on, Buddi," he said, "The race is starting in 30 minutes. We have to get you ready."

Buddi looked back at Alex as he was led away. He felt sick to his stomach and his heart ached. Alex had tears in his eyes but he was waving bravely.

"I'll be watching you, Buddi," Alex said as Buddi left. "Win or lose, you are always number one with me."

Buddi was perplexed. How could Alex think he was number one even if he didn't win? His colleagues didn't think he was that special even when he did win.

He got suited up in his racing jacket and was led through the racetrack where Trophy and the other dogs were already gathered at the starting gate.

"She looks fast, indeed," Buddi thought.

For some reason, however, he didn't care how fast Trophy was. He kept scanning the audience for Alex and finally saw him sitting with his parents.

Buddi didn't feel the excitement and exhilaration he usually felt right before a race. Suddenly the race didn't matter. All that mattered was his family.

"I have a family who loves me," he thought, "and I'm throwing it away for a race. I've never felt as good winning a race as I do when I curl up with Alex. No one has ever been proud of me the way he is and no one has ever cared for me like mom and dad."

"I love them," Buddi realized. "I can't lose them over this stupid race. I want to go home."

The dogs were in the starting gate. The announcer started to call the race when Buddi did the unthinkable. . .he backed out of the starting gate and forfeited the race. Buddi jumped the fence and and ran into the stands where Alex was sitting. Winning didn't matter. Criticism from the other dogs didn't matter. His family mattered.

"Buddi, do you want to come home?" Alex asked.

Buddi jumped and barked and wagged his tail in response. He thought LeRoy was acting foolishly when he had behaved in such a manner but now it seemed perfectly natural.

Trophy won the race. She approached Buddi after her victory.

"Winning the race is nice but I wish I had a family like yours, Buddi. You are the real winner here."

And he knew that she was right.